Home of the Brave

Allen Say

Houghton Mifflin Company Boston 2002
Walter Lorraine Books

Walter Lorraine *wr* Books

www.houghtonmifflinbooks.com

Library of Congress Cataloging-in-Publication Data

Say, Allen.
  Home of the brave / by Allen Say.
      p. cm.
Summary: Following a kayaking accident, a man experiences the feelings
of children interned during World War II and children on Indian
reservations.
  ISBN 0-618-21223-X
  1. Japanese Americans--Juvenile fiction. 2. Indians of North
America--Juvenile fiction. [1. Japanese Americans--Fiction. 2. Indians
of North America--Fiction. 3. World War, 1939-1945--Evacuation of
civilians--Fiction. 4. Indian reservations--Fiction.] I. Title.
  PZ7.A2744 Ho 2002
  [Fic]--dc21
                                        2001005862

Printed in the United States of America
WOZ 10 9 8 7 6 5 4 3 2 1

For Maria-San

When the man came to the mouth of the
gorge, he set his boat down. He stood still and
listened to the river, then slowly pushed
out onto the dark water.

The riffles turned to waves and the waves turned to rapids. The steady roar grew louder. Suddenly the river fell away. The man closed his eyes and held his breath.

The churning water tore away the kayak
and paddle, his helmet and life jacket. When
at last he took a breath, he was being swept
into an underground river.
His strength and hope draining, he imagined
seeing a faint light. Slowly it grew brighter.

The tunnel widened into a large cave lit by a single shaft of light. He did not see the ladder until he crawled out of the water. He climbed up.

At the top he looked out onto a desert. Some
ruined buildings made of earth stood nearby.
Must be an Indian reservation, he thought.
Two dark figures crouched against an adobe wall
caught his eye. He walked toward them.

He was surprised to see that they were two
small children.

"What are you doing here?" he asked.

"Waiting to go home," the girl answered.

"How did you get here?" he asked.

"From the camp," she said.

"And where is your home?" he asked.

They did not answer.

He leaned down and looked at the tags on their coats.

He could not make out the writing.

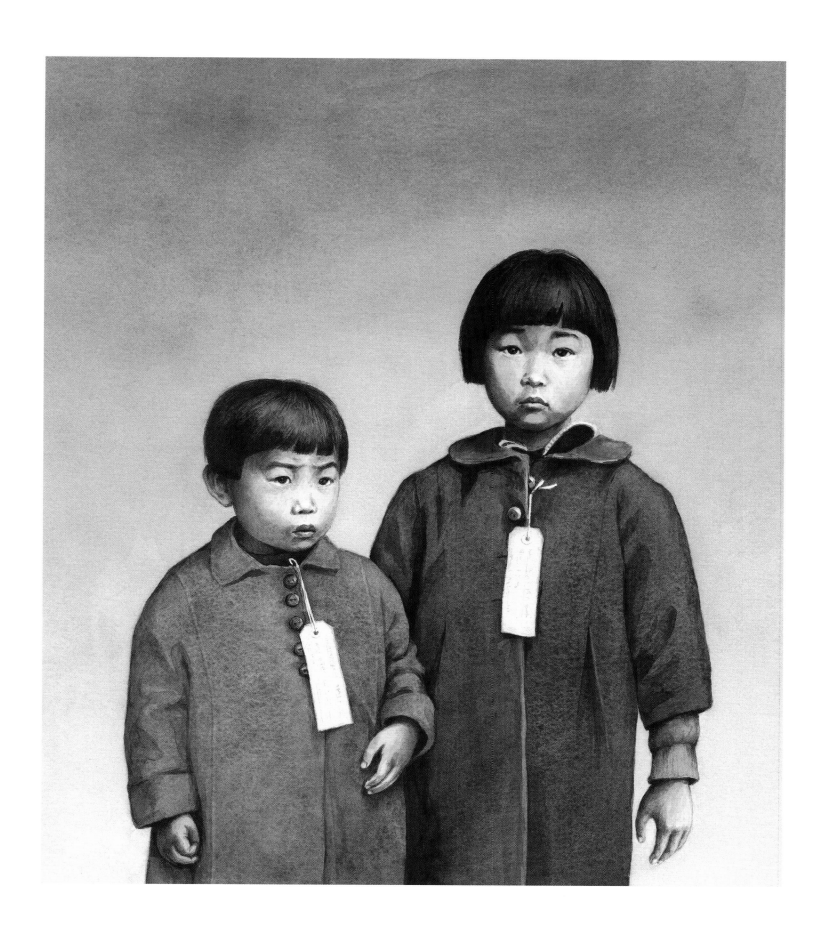

"Looks like we are lost together," he said.
"Come, there must be a town somewhere."
He took their hands and together they walked
into the desert.
They did not walk long before a wind
began to blow, filling the air with dust.
"Close your eyes!" the man yelled, pulling the
children forward. After a time he shouted, "Lights!
I see lights! A town!"

They came to a row of buildings made of wood
and tarpaper. All the windows were dark.
"Camp," the children said.
He looked at them, and they looked away.
"Let's see if anybody's here," he said.
They shook their heads.
"But I saw the lights," he said. "I'll be right back."
Alone he walked to the nearest house.

"Hello," the man called through an open door.
No one answered.
He went up the steps and looked into a small
room. It was empty except for a piece of paper
lying on the floor. It was a nametag, like the ones
the girls wore. He went in and picked it up.
"No!" he cried. The tag had his name on it.
He stood still as if stricken, then a sound
startled him. He rushed outside.

A group of children stood before him like one
large body with many eyes. They stared in silence.
Then all at once the small mouths opened.
"Take us home!" they chanted.
"Get back inside!" A tremendous voice boomed.
Everyone turned. Behind them, two watchtowers
loomed in the darkening sky.
"Get back inside!" the loudspeakers bellowed again.
The children started to run.

Like swords, two beams of light slashed
at the children.
"Turn them off! Turn them off!" he shouted at
the watchtowers.
The searchlights turned to him and blinded him.
He staggered after the sound of running feet.

When he could see again, the children were
gone. Before him was a round pit like an arena.
In the middle was a hole, with a ladder.
A single nametag lay nearby. It had a girl's
name on it — the same as his mother's.
And now he remembered he had been
named after his mother's father. As he put
the tag with the other in his pocket, he thought
he heard voices of children inside the hole.
He climbed down.
At the bottom was complete darkness.
"Where are you?" he called.
Only echoes of his own voice answered.
A great weariness came over him.
He lay down and fell asleep.

Whispering voices woke him. He was lying by the side of a river. A group of children were standing by a boat on the bank. With a start he realized that it was his kayak.

"You didn't have to run," he said. They turned and stared. They were not the same children.

"Where am I?" he asked.

"You're in our camp," one of them answered.

"No!" he exclaimed. He sat up and saw the pieces of paper on the ground. Nametags.

He leapt to his feet and ran up the bank.

A gust of wind scattered the tags in the air.
The man took the two tags from his pocket and
released them. The strips of paper joined the
others. Suddenly the cloud of nametags seemed to
turn into a great flock of birds. The man and the
children watched until they disappeared
over the mountains.
"They went home," said a child.
"Yes, they went home," the man said.
And the children nodded.

During the retrospective show of my work at the
Japanese American National Museum in Los Angeles,
I had the opportunity to see its exhibition of the
World War II internment camps in the United States.
Some facts and numbers were familiar to me — more
than 120,000 Japanese Americans interned in ten camps
in six western states — but now the statistics took on a
human face and voice. I stared and listened. And what
I saw and heard turned into yet another personal
journey. This is that story.

Allen Say

ML

4/02